# JUST AN AIRPLANE

## BY GINA AND MERCER MAYER

Reader's Digest **Kids**

Westport, Connecticut

We went on a trip. We had to fly
on an airplane. My sister and I were
excited—we had never been on an
airplane before.

We left early the morning of the trip
so we'd have plenty of time. We didn't
want the plane to leave without us.

It was a good thing we left early.
There was lots of traffic.

By the time we got to the airport, it was
almost time for our plane to take off.
We had to run all the way through
the airport.

But it was okay because our plane
was late, too.

We had time for breakfast, so we ate
at a restaurant with big windows.
We watched planes taking off and landing.
Then it was time to board our plane.

When we got to our gate, they were just calling our flight. They let us go on first because we had a baby.

Mom and Dad and the baby sat together.
My sister and I sat across the aisle.
We got our seat belts all tangled up.

Then the plane started moving.
It was really slow at first,
but it got faster and faster.
Then it took off into the sky.

As the plane climbed, my ears felt weird.
There were clouds right outside of the window.
And everything on the ground looked so tiny.

I guess my baby brother's ears felt weird, too.
He started crying.

He cried when we were having our lunch.

He cried through the movie.

He cried when Dad walked around with him.

When it was almost time to land, the baby
fell asleep. I think everyone was glad.

When the plane landed, it made a screeching
sound. It was speeding fast down the runway.
Then the plane slowed down and the pilot parked
it at the gate—just like a car.

As we were leaving the plane, the flight attendant asked, "Would you like to see the cockpit and meet the crew?" Mom and Dad said we could.

We met the pilot and the copilot and
the navigator. They let us sit in their seats
and try on their hats. The pilot gave us
coloring books to keep.

Then it was time to get off the plane. Mom and Dad were ready to leave, but I wasn't. I wanted to ride in the plane again!

Mom said, "Don't worry, we have to
take a plane to get home."

Going on a trip is fun, but flying
in an airplane is the most fun of all.